Billy and the Brilliant Babysitter

Billy and the Brilliant Babysitter

HIAWYN ORAM

ILLUSTRATED BY
SONIA HOLLEYMAN

ORCHARD BOOKS

For Steve
H.O.
For Laura
S.H.

ORCHARD BOOKS
96 Leonard Street, London EC2A 4RH
Orchard Books Australia
14 Mars Road, Lane Cove, NSW 2066
ISBN 1 85213 696 0 (hardback)
ISBN 1 85213 857 2 (paperback)
First published in Great Britain 1994
First paperback publication 1995
Text © Hiawyn Oram 1994
Illustrations © Sonia Holleyman 1994
The right of Hiawyn Oram to be identified as the Author
and Sonia Holleyman as the Illustrator of this Work
has been asserted by them in accordance with the
Copyright, Designs and Patents Act, 1988.
A CIP catalogue record for this book is available from the British Library.
Printed in Belgium

Billy's mother and father were going out. Billy
didn't like them going out. He specially didn't like
them going to a fancy dress ball.

His mother was going as Boadicea, the warrior queen.
His father was going as an American gangster with
a false gold tooth and a huge fake cigar.

Billy lay on the bed watching them put the finishing touches to their costumes. He didn't need to close his eyes to see his father, with four other gangsters in gangster hats, driving to America.

He didn't need to half-close his eyes to see his mother in a chariot riding off into the hills.

"I thought that, when I was little," she went on telepathically. "But I was wrong. And you're wrong. Why, right this minute your mother and father are

getting out of their car and walking up the path to
the fancy dress ball behind a Big Brown Bear and a
Goldilocks."

Billy didn't even need to close his eyes to see it.

"And now they're saying hello to Billy the Kid, not you of course, a grown-up Kid, and a Fairy from the top of a Christmas tree and a can of Tomato Soup with legs.

Billy didn't even need to blink to see it.

"And now they're sitting down at a table with a

Chess Piece and the Queen of Hearts, a Highwayman and a Bookworm. The Bookworm is leaning over to your mother and saying, 'Pat, can Billy come to play on Saturday?'"

"That'll be my friend Joe's mother," said Billy, not needing to think twice to see it.

"And now your mother and father are getting up to dance. They're whirling and twirling round the dance floor. And now they've changed partners and

your father is dancing with the Bookworm and your
mother is dancing with the Chess Piece..."
"That'll be Joe's dad," said Billy. "He's chess-mad."